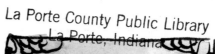

For my mum and dad
—E. S.

For RJ and Will
—K. S.

A FEIWEL AND FRIENDS BOOK
An imprint of Macmillan Publishing Group, LLC
120 Broadway, New York, NY 10271

OLD MACDONALD HAD A BABY. Text copyright © 2019 by Emily Snape.
Illustrations copyright © 2019 by K-Fai Steele. All rights reserved.

Printed in China by RR Donnelley Asia Printing Solutions Ltd., Dongguan City, Guangdong Province.

Our books may be purchased in bulk for promotional, educational, or business use.
Please contact your local bookseller or the Macmillan Corporate and Premium Sales Department at
(800) 221-7945 ext. 5442 or by email at MacmillanSpecialMarkets@macmillan.com.

Library of Congress Cataloging-in-Publication Data
Names: Snape, Emily, author. | Steele, K-Fai, illustrator.
Title: Old MacDonald had a baby / Emily Snape ; illustrated by K-Fai Steele.
Description: First edition. | New York : Feiwel and Friends, 2019. | Summary:
New father Old MacDonald spends a day caring for his baby,
with a little help from the farm animals.
Identifiers: LCCN 2019001973 | ISBN 9781250302816 (hardcover)
Subjects: | CYAC: Stories in rhyme. | Babies—Fiction.
Classification: LCC PZ8.3.S6724 Old 2019 | DDC [E]—dc23
LC record available at https://lccn.loc.gov/2019001973

The artwork was created with watercolor and ink.
Feiwel and Friends logo designed by Filomena Tuosto
First edition, 2019 / Book design by Rebecca Syracuse and Vera Soki
1 3 5 7 9 10 8 6 4 2
mackids.com

Old MacDonald Had A Baby

Emily Snape   Illustrated by K-Fai Steele

Feiwel and Friends
New York

Old MacDonald had a **baby**,

E-I-E-I-O.

Old MacDonald Had A Baby

Emily Snape   Illustrated by K-Fai Steele

Feiwel and Friends

New York

Old MacDonald had a **baby**,
E-I-E-I-O.

And for that baby he chose some **clothes**,

E-I-E-I-O.

With a **tug-tug** here,
And a
wriggle-wriggle there,

Here's a **sock**,
There's a **sleeve**,
Everywhere a
snap-
snap . . .

Old MacDonald had a baby,

E-I-E-I-O.

And for that baby he made some **food**,

E-I-E-I-O.

With a spoonful **here**,
And a handful **there**,

Here's a **splat**,
There's a **flip**,
Baby's bowl is
upside down . . .

Old MacDonald had a baby,

E-I-E-I-O.

And for that baby he sang a **song**,

E-I-E-I-O.

With a **boom-boom** here,

And a **crash-bang** there,

Here's a **clap**, there's a **whack**,
Everywhere's a raucous ruckus!

Donald had a baby, **E-I-E-I-O.**

Here's a **clap**, there's a **whack**,
Everywhere's a raucous ruckus!

Old MacDonald had a baby, E-I-E-I-O.

Here's a **slide**,
There's a **swing**,
Everywhere's a **gummy grin**.
Old MacDonald had a baby, E-I-E-I-O.

And then that baby, he bumped his **knee**,

E-I-E-I-O.

With a **waa-waa** here,
And a **boo-hoo** there,
Here's a **hug**,
There's a **pat**,
Everywhere's a **"kiss it better. . ."**

Old MacDonald had a baby, E-I-E-I-O.

And for that baby he changed a **diaper**,

E-I-E-I-O.

With a **wipe-wipe** here,
And a **"Stay still!"** there,
"Here's some **cream**,
There we go,"

Everywhere's a **stinky smell.**

Old MacDonald had a baby, E-I-E-I-O.

And for that baby he warmed some **milk**,

E-I-E-I-O.

With a **guzzle-guzzle** here,   and a **slurp-slurp** there,

Here's a **glug**,
There's a **gulp**,

Everywhere's a **big, big**
burp!

Old MacDonald had a baby,

E-I-E-I-O.

And with that baby he built a **tower**,

E-I-E-I-O.

With a **tipple-topple** here,
And another block there,

Here's a **sway**, there's a **swerve**,

Everything comes
crashing down!

Old MacDonald had a baby, E-I-E-I-O.

And for that baby he read a **book**,

E-I-E-I-O.

With a **nursery rhyme** here,

and a **fairy tale** there,

Here's a **chew,** there's a **tug,**
Is there time for **one more hug?**

Old MacDonald had a baby, E-I-E-I-O.

And with that baby he had a **cuddle**, E-I-E-I-O.
With a **big yawn** here,
And a **daddy snuggle** there,
Here's a **squeeze**,
There's a **sigh**,
Everywhere's a **sleepy snooze** . . .

Old MacDonald had a baby,

O-Zzzzzz.